Life

of a

Survivor

By

Victoria Hall

Dedication

Firstly, I want to thank God for giving me the courage to make this book happen. I want to thank my children: Frank Wise, John Harris, Tangela Harris, and Tracey Harris for the support and encouragement when writing this book. I want to thank my sister-in-Christ, Lakeya Guy, with Creatively Unleashed Publishing, LLC. for publishing my book, and also encouraging me to pursue my dream. I will continue writing books and pursuing my dream. Thank you to everyone who will support me by buying my book.

Table of Contents

Chapter One

I was 16 and pregnant, left to take care of a baby who had no father, all by myself and with nobody to help me out with my little boy. Hi, my name is Daytona Diamond Williams, but everyone calls me Day. I grew up in Detroit, Michigan, on West Warren Ave & McKinley Street with my mother and two little brothers. My mother and her family were also born and raised here in Detroit. I am 5'5", nicely built for my age, with long jet-black hair and a caramel complexion. I look just like my mother, to the point that we can pass for twins. We're the same height, with the same light brown eyes, with the only difference between us being that she has curly dark hair with a darker complexion, and her skinny build, all due to the usage of drugs.

Today, I want to tell you how I survived through it all. I fell in love with my high school sweetheart. I ended up pregnant and he left me as soon as he found out. All I wanted was to finish high school and go to college, but, as you can see, that never happened. Needless to say, I got my GED, but let me tell you my story from the beginning. I grew up in a poor family, with my mother and two little brothers, Dakota and Dallas, aged eleven and seven years old respectively. My mother was a drug addict, and from time to time, she would leave us in the house for weeks at a time to take care of ourselves.

During these periods, there would be no food, no heat or hot water in the house. I took care of my brothers the best I could. One day, my mother came home after being out on the streets for a week and a half. I told her that Dallas has been sick for a week now and that I need the insurance card to take him to the doctors. Guess what she said, she had sold the insurance card to some dealer so he could take his son to get some operation that he didn't want to pay for. That left me to go out on the streets at the age of fourteen, and somehow get money to take my little brother to a doctor. So, I did things with men who I didn't even know, just to get the money my baby brother needed to get the care he needed. I did those things so we could eat on days my mother wasn't there.

I was five years old when I was molested by my mother's boyfriend, and not once, but repeatedly. When I said something to my mother about it when I got older, she smacked my face and told me I better not tell that lie to anyone else, so I didn't. The next morning, I got my little brothers dressed, so I can take Dallas to see a doctor. I could do those things as I looked just like a younger version of my mother. My mother was very pretty, even though drugs had taken over her beautiful body. I signed my mother's name on the form so Dallas could be treated, and after that we walked across the street to the drug store for his medicine. As we were walking to the bus stop, I saw that Dallas was getting too weak to walk in the cold, so I picked him up and carried him the rest of the way to the bus stop. When we got home and I put the key in the door to unlock it, I opened the door to see my mother performing sexual activities with a stranger. I hurried up and closed the door so my brothers wouldn't see what was going on. With that sight in mind, I left, and we walked around in the cold for hours with nowhere to go and nothing to do. It is important to remember that I was only fourteen years old and dealing with a situation I couldn't control, all due to my mother's drug problems. I went to a pay phone to call my Aunt Theresa to see if we can come to her house just for the night. To nobody's surprise, she blew me off. She was having a bingo night and didn't want company to ruin her night. Alright, I'll find somewhere else for us to go. We ended up staying in a bus terminal for the night. I couldn't sleep at all, fearing that something would happen to us. When morning came around, we walked home to see if the coast was clear. Once we entered the house, my mother smacked me, hard.

'Mom, why did you hit me, what did I do?' I asked.

'Where were you all night, Daytona? Just because I have company doesn't mean you can come and go as you please.'

I started crying, explaining how she had company and I didn't want to expose my brothers to this sort of company.

'Girl, don't you ever take those boys out of here without me knowing, you hear me!' she screamed in reply.

My lesson learnt, I went to my room and took my little brothers with me. All my mother has to say is how she's going out again. I knew that my mother wasn't coming back for a couple of days, maybe even a couple of weeks. Once I heard the door close, I took some blankets and hung them up on both entrances to the house. I turned on the oven for the heat and put on extra layers of clothing on both me and my brothers to keep us warm. I had only seven dollars to my name so I went to the corner store to get some bread, peanut butter, and jelly for us to eat for a couple of days.

I was very smart for my age, I put a board up at the doors to the house so no one would try to come in, we lived on a street where there was nothing but drugs, robberies, and people with mental illnesses. My brothers and I would sleep in the same bed, and one time, my brothers wanted to sleep while I laid there and cried. I was so afraid that someone would break in and hurt us, so I slept with a kitchen knife under my pillow.

Everyone on the block knew my mother, but despite this I didn't trust anybody. After all, I had been abused by my mother and all her boyfriends. I always told my brothers that no matter what, I would never leave their side. As the nights went on, I would read school books for homework that was due in the morning. I was a straight A student in school, and very smart. I had fallen in love with this boy in my school, Lance Mitchel. Lance was sixteen years old, almost six feet with dark skin, dreads, and a tattoo of a snake on his neck. Lance played on the football team for the school.

Hey Lance, I texted him. He didn't reply so I texted him again, asking if he was free. He never texted back. Lance and I had been talking to each other for six months, and in this time period, he had always answered every call and text that I sent him, but this time, he just didn't answer. I could only lay there, holding on to my brothers until the sun came up.

The alarm on my phone went off, so I got up and got ready for school. I had to be at school by 7:15am and my brothers had to reach their school by 8:45am. My mother never came home last night, but I already expected this. So, I had to ask the next-door neighbor to put my brothers on the bus with her kids. My bus came and I didn't see Lance on the bus.

Once I got to school, one of my friends showed me a video of Lance and some girl named Katelyn. They were kissing, and Lance was rubbing all on this girl. I will admit, I was hurt as I really liked Lance and I thought that he liked me too. I went off to my first class, one that Lance was supposed to be in with me, but he didn't show up to class that day. After class was over, I called him, but again he didn't answer. I called him again and it went to voicemail.

It was the end of the school day, and I still hadn't seen or heard from Lance. I didn't think anything of it, he might just be absent today. That's when I logged onto my Facebook account, and a picture of Lance and Katelyn was the first thing that greeted me. I'm not going to lie, I wanted to confront them both, but I calmed myself down and decided to wait and see if he would come to me.

My friend Brianna was there with me, looking at this picture. We lived two doors over from each other and we also grew up together. Our mothers were close friends and did drugs with each other. Brianna had two older sisters that lived there with her and her mother. Brianna was also 5"5 with shoulder length hair, black eyes and a nose ring. Brianna was also very pretty, and she had all the boys in school going wild over her.

"So, Brianna, what do you think I should do about this, do you think I should confront them, or what?"

"I don't know, you've got a lot going on right now at home, I really don't think you should let this boy worry you. And Day, he's no good for you anyway. He lies to you all the time; he doesn't post pictures of you both on social media, but he'll post a picture of this girl, Katelyn, and him. Why should you put yourself through all of this, just for this boy?"

Brianna was right, but I was in love with Lance and would hear nothing against him. What Brianna didn't know was that I believed everything Lance would tell me, even if I knew it was a lie. As we were getting on the bus, I realized that Brianna knew I was hurt. I tried not to let her see the tears in my eyes.

The bus pulled up at the corner of our block when my phone rang. It was Lance. Once Brianna went to her house, I walked to the corner store just so I could pick up the phone.

"Hey, Lance, I missed you in school today."

"Yeah, I have a cold, that's why I was absent today," he replied. I just looked at my phone in disbelief, but I played along with it.

"Can I come see you tonight?" I asked him.

"Nah, Day that isn't a good idea, I have a twenty-four hour bug and I don't want to get you sick," he said.

"No problem," I said, "will I see you in school tomorrow?"

"Yeah, I should be there."

"Alright, I hope you feel better, Lance." All I heard in reply was a click on the other end, he didn't even say thank you or goodbye.

Brianna was right; he was rude and he didn't care about me or my feelings, but I love him. I walked up the street to my house when I saw my mother pulling up in a cab.

"Day, come help me take these bags into the house," she said. I look inside, and they were filled with food, but I knew it wasn't from a store. She must have went to one of the food banks again. I helped her with the bags, and as I was walking into the house, I saw something happening down the corner. A man was waving a gun in this other guy's face, telling him how he should kill him cause the man had beat the other's sister up.

"Go in the house and mind your own business," my mother said, as we were closing the door. Suddenly, I heard a popping sound. It sounded like a firecracker but I knew a gun had fired, as it was a sound we were all familiar with. This was the life that the hood had given us.

Chapter Two

It was 3:45pm and my brothers were about to get off the school bus. I walked to the door and could hear sirens sounding in the street. My mother pulled me back in the house and said that she will get Dakota and Dallas off the bus. I wondered what she was up to, so I peek out the window and see her telling Brianna's mom that Rich, the man who got shot, was beating on Tony's, the gunman, sister again, and that's why Tony shot him. The police pulled up, but Tony had already left, and nobody told them where he went, or what had happened, as you don't snitch in this neighborhood. Not if you cared about your life.

My mother sent my brothers to the house after they got off the bus. Dallas had asked a lot of questions about what was going on out there. I told him how people will do terrible things to other people, and sometimes they must pay for it. I promised my brothers that I will make sure that they will not be living like this for long. Once I got out of school, I would come back to take them from my mother. My brothers meant a lot to me, and I wanted only the best for them.

My mother came into the house and told me that some boy wanted me outside. It was Lance. My mom interrogated me about him, asking if I had had sex with him before she let me go.

I went outside to see him and we talked, now I told you I believe everything that Lance tells me because I was in love with this boy and I wanted to be his girlfriend no matter what.

"Lance, are you and Katelyn in a relationship? If so, where do we stand?" I asked him.

"Day, I'm not in a relationship with anyone. I told you before, I can do what I want, and with whomever I want to do it with."

"Alright, Lance, you're right. We are just friends, and I need to remember that. So, what brings you here today, Lance?"

"Day, I just wanted to clear things up about the stuff that was said about Katelyn and me on social media. Yes, I hugged her, I kissed her, and that was all. My boys dared me to do it, so I did it."

This boy had the nerve to laugh while telling me this.

"Lance, it's alright, I believe you. I'm not worried about what people say because I know one day, we will be together."

"Day, I'm only telling you this because I don't want your feelings to be hurt. I know you really like me, but I'm not ready for a relationship with anyone."

All I could say was, "alright, I'll talk to you later," before I walked in the house with tears in my eyes.

I ran in the bathroom and started vomiting, but I couldn't let my mother find out. I had missed my period for the last 2 months, and I was scared to tell my mother. I called Brianna and asked her if she could run to the corner store and grab me a pregnancy test.

"Girl, don't tell me you got pregnant by that boy. You've only been together a couple of times. Your mother is going to kill you."

"Brianna, I know, and I think I am two months in. What am I going to do? I can't afford an abortion, and neither can my mother, even if I do tell her I am pregnant."

"Day, whatever choice you make, I will support you all the way. I'm your best friend and I'm here for you."

I started crying. I didn't know what to do, I couldn't take care of myself, let alone a baby. Brianna told me that I should tell my mother, despite my apprehensions.

"Brianna, you're right, I will tell her, but I need to talk to Lance and tell him that I am carrying his baby."

After I hung up, I called Lance, and to my surprise he answered the phone on the 1st ring.

"Hello," he said, and I choked up before I could reply.

"Hey Lance, this is Day. I have something to tell you. Lance, I took a pregnancy test, and it was positive. It got real quiet on the phone. "Hello," I said, "Lance, say something please."

"Day, are you sure that it's my baby?" he asked.

As I was telling him that I hadn't been with anyone else, I heard a click and then a dial tone, he had hung up on me. I just sat there with tears in my eyes, I was very hurt when he tried telling me that the baby I was carrying wasn't his.

I called Brianna back and told her what Lance had said and how he hung up on me. That's when I heard a knock on my door, it was my mother. I bade Brianna a quick farewell after telling her that my mother was here.

"Day, who was that boy?" asked my mother. "And why would he come to my house?"

At first, I just looked at her, then she yelled, "DAYTONA, I ASKED YOU A QUESTION! Answer me."

"His name is Lance, and he goes to my school. We are just friends," I said.

"Day, if I found out that you're lying or hiding something I'll take a belt to you and I mean it.

My mother was no joke. She was a fighter out in the streets of Detroit and her name rang bells out here. If I told my mother, she would throw me out of the house. I just sat there and cried.

As the months went on, my birthday, December 1st, drew near. Lance and I grew apart from each other. He stopped calling me, he stopped answering my calls and texts, he even changed his cell phone number. He blocked me on every social media site there is. Lance took my love for granted and it broke my heart. I started skipping school so I wouldn't see him with other girls. I lost a lot of weight, to the point that people thought I was on drugs, like my mother. I lost so much weight you couldn't even tell I was six months pregnant.

I called Brianna to come over because I needed someone to talk to. I had to get my life back in order, not only for myself but also for my brothers. I told her what was going on between Lance and I, and she told me to get an abortion. That, however, was out of the question, and I told her as much. At this point, the stress had reached such a level that I couldn't help but cry and vomit while talking to her.

Brianna talked me into going back to school, but I was skeptical about going back as I didn't want to see what was coming my way with Lance and his new girlfriend. On my first day back, it felt like everyone was laughing at me. I was at my locker when my neighborhood friend Julie came up.

"Hey Julie," I said.

"Hey girl," she replied with a look on her face. Julie went on to tell me about all the rumors Lance had been spreading about me. He was telling people that I was pregnant and that I claimed that the baby was his. I sighed and told her I couldn't control what Lance was saying.

"Day, are you keeping the baby?" asked Julie.

"I am six months in, I am going to have my baby. Lance doesn't have to be in this baby's life, I'm just so over all of this, Julie. I cried so much, not knowing how to tell my mother that I was pregnant. Lance doesn't want to have anything to do with me or the baby. I know that my mother will throw me out and I'm not going to have anywhere to live. My mind is racing all over the place right now. I'm worried about my little brothers, leaving them there with my mother. Julie, I don't know what will happen with them if I leave them there with her. I don't even know if they will eat or have clean clothes," I cried, when Brianna walked over.

"Hey, what's going on," she said. I lifted my head up and tears were streaming down my eyes.

"Oh my God, Day," she says, as she looks at me and then Julie. Julie shrugged her shoulders as I fell into Brianna's arms crying. I need my girls right now. I needed Lance more than anything right now.

Chapter Three

School was over, but instead of getting on the bus, Brianna, Julie, and I walked home from school. I knew my friends meant well about everything that they told me and were only trying to help. But I really needed to tell my mother that I was pregnant.

I walked in the door and my mother was standing there with a trash bag at her side. She looked like she was crying but was also mad.

"Daytona, when were you going to tell me that you were pregnant? Day, that's a question and I want an answer," she said, now starting to yell.

"Mom, I didn't know how to tell you, I've been thinking about it all day in school. I'm sorry I let this happen."

"Well, you know what, Daytona? I'm sorry too because you can no longer stay here in my house. I cannot afford to take care of another person. I told you not to get pregnant the day you were out there talking with that boy outside, and you did exactly what I told you not to do."

She threw the trash bag at me and told me to get out, so I left, and I knew I could never stay with my mother again. I stayed at Julie's for a few nights as I could keep a watch out for my little brothers who my mom would still leave alone from time to time. I had to figure out what I was going to do or where I was going to go next. But I knew that I had to do something because I couldn't leave my brothers under the same roof as my addict mother.

I was at Julie's for about two weeks when Julie's mother told me that it was time for me to go. I had to find somewhere else to stay. Julie told me that her mother and my mother had gotten into an argument about me staying at her house. I couldn't go to Brianna's house as she lived two doors over from us and my mother would have a problem with me being there as well. So, I took the little bit of money that I had saved up and went to a shelter for a couple of months.

While I was staying in the shelter, I went into labor and they had to rush me to the hospital. I gave birth on the 3rd of March to a baby boy. He was perfect, I fell in love with him as soon as I saw his face, he was so handsome. When I left the hospital, I lied and told them I had a place to go so they wouldn't try and take Lance Jr from me. Brianna and Julie were there every day, visiting me. I was hoping that my mother was coming to see her only grandson, but she never came or called to see how we were doing. Julie's mother picked me up from the hospital and took me to a shelter she stayed at when she had nowhere to go. I ended up staying in the shelter for 9 months until I met James, the nightmare of my life.

December 1st came, and it was now my seventeenth birthday. My son was now nine months old, and I hadn't seen my little brothers in months. I hadn't heard anything from Lance in a year or so, I hadn't been in school and this was supposed to be my last year of school. I met this guy while I was in the shelter, he was one of the meal carriers, and worked for Burger King. We got to know each other, each time he brought food over to the shelter we would talk to each other.

As the months went on, we started seeing each other. He asked me to come and stay with him at his house, but I couldn't as I really didn't know him well enough to go and stay at his place. His name was James, and he was eight years older than me. James got me a job at Burger King on the East side of Warren Ave. The only position they had for me was on the night shift. I had to get Brianna to watch my son for me three nights out of the week, while Julie watched him the other two nights. I worked as much as I could so I can get my own apartment for me and my brothers.

My first day at work was good, but I did not know that James was a manager there. After work James dropped me off at Brianna's house, but it was late and I knew that her mother wouldn't let me stay there, so I walked seven blocks with my son to the shelter, but that was full. I called James and asked if my son and I could stay with him for the night as the shelters were all filled up. He came to the shelter, picked me up and we went to his house, where he showed me where me and my son were going to sleep. I put my bag in the room and put my son to sleep. James and I stayed up talking and getting to know each other. James was a nice guy; he took me and my son out to dinner a few nights of the week. He took us shopping and we stayed at his house whenever the shelter was full.

The next two weeks we went to work, I looked at my work schedule for the week. I realized that I only worked the days and hours that James worked. After work, we would go back to his place, a three bedroom house on Thornhill Street, in a nice neighborhood, totally different from where I was from.

As soon as we got in the house, he started asking me questions about my son and the father. I gave him a look, wondering what was with all the questions, and I didn't really want to talk to him about Lance Sr yet. I didn't really think it was any of his business at the time.

I got up to sleep in the room with my son when James told me I could sleep in his room. Granted, this man got me a job where he works, but I knew him for barely three months. He was a nice guy but he was too controlling, and I'm just not into someone controlling me. I've been through a lot in my seventeen years and I was not going to let this man control everything I do and say. I was adamant on sleeping in the same room as my son, and I let James know that.

"Fine, he can sleep in the room with us," he said, with an attitude. We laid down in the bed but James was so mad that he ended up sleeping on the couch. The next morning, James cooked me breakfast. He made French toast, eggs, bacon, and sausage patties with a tall glass of orange juice. To my surprise the food looked good, and tasted even better.

"Hey James, can I please get a ride to the library?" I asked.

"What are you going to do at the library?"

"I want to look up some classes so I can take my GED, if that's alright with you."

"Day, I just want to help you, I know some people that run a GED class."

"Okay, if you can help me get into one of the classes I would really appreciate it. Since I can't finish high school, I want to get my GED so I can have a better life for my son and little brothers."

"Day, I would love for you and your son to come and stay with me so you'll not have to go from shelter to shelter or try to look for somewhere to sleep at night. It's cold outside and at least you will have a warm spot to sleep at."

"James, let me think about it, I'll let you know later."

"Day, I'm only trying to help. I know it's hard to take care of a young child at your age so all I want to do is help you out," he said.

James called his friend about the GED classes, but he didn't have any available spots open for me. He said that he will inform me once he has a spot open. That was okay as it would give me more time to save money to move into my own place.

"Hey, James, can you run me over to my little brothers' school so I can see them? I haven't seen my brothers in nine months, and I really miss them."

James took me to their school, I waited outside for them to get on the bus, but they never came out of the school. I asked their teacher if they were in school today and she told me that they haven't been in school for a couple of days. I tried calling my mother but she didn't pick up and now I was worried about my brothers. I got back in the car and James saw the look on my face.

"Day, is everything alright?" he asked.

"No," I replied, "can you please take me to my mother's house."

We got to the house, and I can see my mother outside talking with Brianna's mother. I get out of the car, and you should have seen the look on her face. I hadn't seen my mother since she put me out.

"Hey mom," I said, as I walked up to her to give her a hug. Tears came to my eyes as I got closer to her, my mother was fading away so bad, I couldn't stand to see her like that.

"Hey, Day, how are you doing?" she asked. "I see you're looking good there, what brings you back this way?"

"I'm not here to stay with you mom, I just want to see Dakota and Dallas, that's all. I just want to make sure they're alright, that's all."

So, she went in the house and brought the boys out. Dallas ran and jumped in my arms while Dakota wrapped his arms around my legs. I asked them why they hadn't been going to school and they told all about how they were being treated at home. My mother had been severely neglecting them.

Tears immediately came to my eyes, but it was time to go. It broke my heart that I had to leave my little brothers with my mother. I got back into the car and James asked me what happened. I told him how my mother was not sending the boys to school and that she had been leaving them in the house by themselves.

"They should not be in there alone in this neighborhood, James," I cried. "I want to take them from her, but I know that my mother is not going to let me just take them from her without a fight, if I take them, that will stop her money and food stamps, both of which I bet the boys never see."

I just sat there, with tears in my eyes watching the house as we drove away. It was like a baby leaving her mother for good, James put his arms around me, and I cried and cried until my stomach started hurting.

"It's going to be alright, he said, "we are going to figure this out, and I am going to help you get your brothers."

It meant a lot to me when he said that. My brothers deserved a life away from my neglectful mother.

Chapter Four

It was now 1 PM and we were on our way home. I told James about my plan to contact Child Protection Services, but he was skeptical, though I managed to convince him.

"Okay Day, I'll help you in any way that you want me to help you with, but it will take time and money and you will need at least a two bedroom apartment. You will need to have money saved up to make sure that you're able to pay your bills and buy food for them. Also, you will need to make sure that you have beds, dressers, and clothes for them. The social workers will ask if you have all of that before they will even get involved in helping you out."

I knew all this, as we were almost taken from my mother when Dallas was 2 years old.

"I always told Dakota and Dallas that I will make a better life for us, and I mean that James," I started crying. "My brothers mean a lot to me, and now I have a son to take care of alone as well."

"James, I need to take off work today please," I asked, "I'm tired, and my eyes are swollen and puffy - I can't work like this."

James begrudgingly agreed, leaving me to wonder why it mattered so much that I had to take a day off work.

When James came back, he started screaming at me, over anything and everything. At first, I didn't try to talk back to him, I thought he was just in a bad mood, but suddenly I lost it. As he berated me for not taking care of my baby, I told him to mind his own business, and that's when he slapped me across the face. He ended up apologizing, blaming it on work, and like a fool, I accepted his apology.

The next morning, I woke up to James cooking breakfast, and he greeted me like nothing happened. I greeted him back, and we talked about the last night. I told him that I did not want him hitting me again, and he apologized for it. I knew I needed his help, so I hoped his apology was sincere. I knew that once a man started abusing a woman, it would never stop, but I hoped it would be different for us. Even though I stayed, I decided to take as much of my matters as I could into my own hands.

However, one day I accepted James' offer to drop Lance off with me. In the car, James started questioning me, this time about one of the workers that we work with. I tried to explain that me and the co-worker in question, Dennis, were only co-workers, and nothing more, but James was not having it.

He smacked me so hard I bit my lip on the inside and it started bleeding. I put my hand up to my mouth to try and stop the bleeding, and all he did was give me a tissue and tell me off for talking back to him.

I thought to myself, I don't have to put up with this. I need to get my son and leave this man, but I also knew I was seventeen years old with a nine month old baby. If I left him, I wouldn't have anywhere to go.

We got out of the car, and James grabbed my arm and told me that I better not tell anyone what he did, otherwise he would go to jail. James had done a lot for me and my son. He took us to his home, he got me a job where he works, and I don't have to pay anything to live with him. I am in love with this man, I can't send him to jail, I thought to myself.

Over my next lunch break, I called my friends Brianna and Julie, just to let them know I was fine and to vent a little about my situation. They were sympathetic to my situation and cared a lot about me. I told them a bit about how much James helped me, and they expressed their concerns about his age, but I told them how much I needed him to take care of us.

"I have some money saved up, but it isn't much. I want to buy a house for my little brothers and myself. I have a plan, but I need James right now, at least until the plan falls through."

"Day, what do you have in your mind now," laughed Brianna. Brianna knew me better than Julie did and she knew when I put a plan together in my head.

"It's nothing - I just need to live with James until I turn 18."

I didn't tell my girls that he was hitting me - at this point I didn't think it was any of their business, so I didn't tell them. I walk back into the job, and I see that Dennis is not at the window of the drive-thru, it looks like Renee is working back there now. I didn't dare ask James what was going on, so I didn't say anything, just went back to work. I later saw Dennis on the grill, right where James can see him, so I just turned back around and kept taking food orders, realizing how much I needed to get away from James.

Work shift was over so we headed over to Julie's to pick Lance Jr up and went on our way home. When we got there, James turned to me.

"I saw you looking around for your boyfriend, Dennis." Before I could say anything, he mugged me so hard that I fell to the ground.

"James, why do you keep putting your hands on me, I told you before that there is nothing going on with Dennis and I."

"I see how you look at him, I see how he tries to look at you too, when I'm not looking. If you want Dennis, then maybe you should go live with Dennis," he said.

"James, I don't want Dennis. I'm here with you. I'm in love with you, not him."

He kicked me in my leg in reply and said, "then act like it," and walked away. I could only lay there with tears rolling down my eyes, not knowing what to say or do at this point.

Next morning, I woke up to the smell of breakfast again. I get Lance Jr and we go down to the kitchen, where James was making breakfast. "You hungry?" he asks. I was scared to say no, so I nodded my head yes. I sat Lance Jr down in his playpen so I could eat with James, who again acted like nothing ever happened, as if he didn't mug me last night. "This food is good, right, Day?" he said.

Again, I shook my head yes, but all I wanted was to throw this hot plate of food in his face, grab my son and run out the door. But where was I going to go? Detroit was a dangerous city and I knew for a fact that being out there with a baby wasn't good.

Chapter Five

James' friends still couldn't get me a GED class, though at this point I thought James was lying about that as well. I had eight thousand dollars saved up as he didn't want me to pay rent or bills in his house. He told me that a man is supposed to take care of his girlfriend while the girl is to take care of the house, but he takes care of both as it's his house so I let him do what he needs to do.

James had no idea what I was going to do with the money. I had seen a house up for thirty thousand dollars, and I planned to buy it for my family. It was just the right size for all of us.

One day, James took me over to the other side of town, where my mother and friends lived. Before I could get out of the car, he grabbed me by the arm.

"James, you're hurting me," I said.

"Day, you better not tell anyone what goes on in this relationship, or you and your son will be out in the cold, you hear me?"

"Yes, James, I hear you. You don't have to worry about me saying anything to anyone."

He kissed me on my cheek before letting go of my arm.

I will be back to pick you up around 8 pm so be ready, OK I will be ready. After I watched him leave, I knocked on Brianna's door and asked her to walk with me to the post office. She told me to leave Lance Jr with Brooke, her oldest sister, and a runaway.

On the way to the post office, Brianna asked me if I had seen my brothers yet.

"No, not yet. Why?" I asked her.

"Day, the cops have been over there twice this week. Your mom and her boyfriend have been fighting. One of the neighbors called the cops when they heard them fighting and your brothers crying."

I stopped in mid tracks and turned around, "wait, what happened? Hold on, Brianna, let me go and check on my mother and my brothers. My mother may not have cared about me, but she will always be my mother, and I am going to always love her."

I ran over to my house and banged on the door. The door unlocked, revealing Dallas, who screamed my name and jumped into my arms. Dakota ran up to me as well, screaming my name.

"Dakota, is mom here?"

"Yes, I'm here Day," she said, laying on the couch.

"Mom, is everything okay? The neighbors told me they heard fighting and kids crying over here."

"Day, everything is okay. I had to put Robert out of the house. The man tried to bring another girl into my house."

"Okay, I just wanted to make sure that you're alright. Would it be okay if I take the boys out to get something to eat?"

"Yes, go ahead. They haven't eaten anything all morning. I wasn't feeling good enough to get up and cook anything."

I took my brothers to a restaurant two blocks down the street. I got them enough to fill their little bellies up. I also got them some bread, peanut butter, and jelly so they could eat on the days that my mother is not home. Dallas's little hands were shaking so we went next door and I got them both some gloves, hats, and scarves from the poppy store.

I told the boys not to let my mother see what I had got them, and we decided to go see my son, their nephew.

We got to Brianna's house and as soon as I opened the door, Dakota ran into the house and picked his nephew up and started hugging him. I let the boys spend an hour with him, and then I took them back home with my mother. I knew James was coming back soon to pick us up, so I had to hurry and walk to the post office and put the money into my post office box before he got here.

As soon as we walked back from around the corner, I saw James pulling up. I gave my girls a hug and got into the car. On the way back, James started an argument with me again, this time about why I came to this side of town every weekend. I tried to tell him that I came to see my friends and brothers, who I hadn't talked to for a long time.

He didn't say anything the rest of the way home, but had this mean look on his face. I'm not going to lie, I was scared, I thought that as soon as we got into the house, he was going to hit me. I couldn't tell anyone because he told me if I said anything to anyone, he would hurt me badly and put my son and me out in the cold. If he did that, I knew we wouldn't be able to survive, so I had no other choice but to put up with him and his beatings.

We got home and I was taking my time getting the baby out of the car, so James started yelling at me, telling me to hurry up. We get inside the house, and he starts asking me all these questions again. I tried to explain my reasons again but he hit me and told me that next time, he would pick them up and bring them home for me to meet.

After I had laid Lance Jr down, James resumed hitting me, punching me in the face, stomach, and head, as I curled up on the floor, crying. He walked out the door and slammed it, waking up my son who started screaming. I held him rocking, knowing we had to get out of here.

The next day came about, and I told James that I couldn't go to work as I had a black eye and couldn't go out of the house with such an injury. He cooked my breakfast and told me he had to do some chores before going to work. I nodded my head and he kissed me and walked out the door. I waited a while before I made my moves, I looked up some GED classes and found one that James didn't know anything about. I called the instructor and set up an appointment to speak with someone to take some classes, I explained my situation with my son, and was told that they have a daycare in the building.

Now that I got that out of the way, the appointment is in two months, so that will give me some time to get a plan together on how I am going to go every day, without James knowing about it.

All I could think about during James' absence was how he had abused me. He would rape me if I refused sex, he didn't care if my son was in the room, he'd still hit me. All I could wish for was for time to speed up so I could turn eighteen and leave.

Three hours had already gone by since James left the house, I knew he had to be to work for another hour. That's when he called me to apologize for the black eye he gave me. I tried to control my temper as he said, "Day, I don't want you to leave me." He sounded like he was crying. "James, I'm not leaving," I said back to the man that gave me the black eye that kept me at home.

James told me that he'd let the manager know of my absence before telling me he'd gotten me something. Once the call ended, I took care of things at home and with my son and went to sleep. When I woke up, James was standing over me, yelling at me for ignoring his calls. He started beating me, with the 'gift' he'd brought back, which were flowers. Some of the flowers came out of the bouquet and landed on my son, all as I yelled for James to stop.

After it was over, he got up, kicked me, and told me to clean myself up. I cried so hard I felt my veins almost pop out of my head. I tried to quiet my son, but when I looked at him, he had a slight cut on his cheek. I cleaned his face and held him close, telling him that we would get out of here soon, real soon. I finally got Lance Jr to sleep, and took a shower so I could get ready for bed. When I walked into the bedroom, James wasn't in the bed, he wasn't even in the room. I walked into the kitchen and I saw him on facetime, talking to Sheila from work. I stood there, listening to his conversation with her. I thought to myself, this is why he keeps beating on me because he is cheating on me with this lady.

As I was walking back into the living room, I heard James call me, "Day! Were you listening to my conversation?"

"No, James, I just came down here to get the baby a bottle of milk," I said.

"Because if you did, that was Sheila from work. She was asking where they keep the extra kids meal boxes at."

I decided to run with it as I didn't want any more beatings. He walked past me and bumped me as he went upstairs to the bedroom. I just stood there with a hurt look on my face, asking myself how I ended up in this mess with this man anyway.

After a few hours went by, I went upstairs to get in the bed, but James told me to sleep with my son, without even looking in my direction. I decided to follow his commands and sleep in the other room. The next morning, I hear James screaming my name from downstairs. I jumped up, shaking off my sleep and ran to the ground floor. He had Lance Jr in his arms and was screaming at the top of his lungs, I snatched my son out of his arms and checked to make sure that he didn't have any marks on his body or anything.

"Why are you checking him, Day?" he said, "I didn't hurt him, I would never hurt your son. I love him as if he were mine."

James cooked breakfast as usual, like nothing happened the night before. So, we ate breakfast, I gave the baby a bath, laid him down and then I took a shower. It was now 11:30 am, we had to go across town to drop Lance Jr off at Julie's house so we could go to work. Before we left, James came into the room with some roses in his hand. "Here,

Day. I bought these for you," he said. I gave a slight smile and thanked him, but he gave me a look and said, "what, don't you want them?"

I told him I wanted them, as I put them in a jar with some water, and we left the house. We dropped the baby off, but James kept complaining about how dropping Lance off was wasting his time.

"Day, I found someone to watch him. She will watch him at the house while you're at work. She lives close by and is willing to do it for you, I'll pay her."

Now my mind is racing. James has not done anything for my son since we moved in here. All he did was take us places, but to say that he is going to pay for a babysitter just so I won't go into town, something else was going on.

I asked James who this person was, and to my surprise he said it was Sheila. I was enraged, how could I leave my son with someone I didn't know? Plus, James was going to change our shifts to further inconvenience me. When I voiced my opinions, James smacked me so hard I thought I had gone deaf for a moment.

We pulled up to the job with me still feeling dizzy. When James stopped the car, he got out and opened the door for me. As we walked up to the job, James grabbed me by my arm and said, "I better not catch you talking to anyone in here, Day. I hired you to work, not to be in anyone's face."

Now let me tell you this: I did everything that this man told me to do, and I was scared of him, but I had nowhere to go as my mother wouldn't let me come home and I couldn't stay with any of my friends so I took all of the abuse, physically, mentally, and emotionally.

I saw that Bruce the General Manager was here today, so I kind of felt safe as James knew not to do anything wrong while Bruce was here. I looked around for Dennis, but I didn't see him, but James saw me looking around, and though he didn't say anything, I knew something would happen on our way back from work. I went on about my business and did my work when Bruce called me over to his office. He offered me a change in positions, to be specific, he was offering a managerial position. The timings would suit me and the pay was more as well, so I agreed.

When I walked out of the office, I saw James looking at me. He called me over and asked me what Bruce wanted so I told him. He gave me a look, as if I had to ask him before taking the position.

It was now 11 o'clock and our shift was over, so we clocked out for the night. As we walked to the car, James said to me, "you better not be taking that position, Day."

I didn't say anything, so he grabbed me by my arm, and said, "did you hear what I just said to you?"

"Yes, I heard you, and yes, I am taking the position."

Before I could get another word out of my mouth, he punched me in the mouth so hard my lip started bleeding, but he didn't stop. He hit me again and again. I fell to the ground and curled up into a ball, covering my face. He started kicking me in my back and side. If it wasn't for a man passing by pulling him off me, James would have broken every rib I had in my body. He told me to get up and get in the car but the man asked if I was alright and if I wanted him to call the police. I said no and got into the car holding my side and crying. We pulled up to the house and he pulled me out of the car and dragged me into the house, throwing me to the floor. He told me to call Brianna and tell her that we were getting off work at 12 and that he will pick the baby up by 12:30. James repeatedly raped me over and over, until it was time for him to go pick my son up. I didn't want my son to see me in pain or the bruises I had on my face and hands from him dragging me on the ground. He got up, spit on me and left the room, while I laid there crying out for my mother, but I knew that she couldn't help me.

I heard the front door close, I got up, went to the bathroom, took a shower and cleaned myself up, before he got back with Lance Jr.

Chapter Six

Today was the first day that I started my new position, and I was so excited. My hours were from 7am to 4pm, which gave me time to drop Lance off at the daycare as well as pick him up if I had to catch the bus there. James was not happy at all, as now I could see what was going on with him and Sheila. James used to work the nightshift with me, but a week before Bruce asked me to become a manager, James had switched his shift to day shift to be with Sheila. I didn't care about them; all I needed was a place to stay until I turned eighteen. It was so funny to see the look on their faces when I walked into the job looking nice and clean, I had gotten my hair done and was looking like a movie star. James almost dropped the fries that he just pulled up. Now I'm thinking him and Sheila were a couple because she had an attitude when she saw the way he was looking at me.

I went into the office where Bruce was, he gave me instructions on what I had to do. First, I switched out all the cashiers from the overnight shift and replaced the drawers with the morning shift crew. James couldn't believe I took the position and how good I looked in my uniform. I saw him blow me a kiss at one point, but I rolled my eyes at him. I looked at James with disgust in my eyes as Sheila was a big girl, I mean she had to weigh at least two hundred and seventy-five pounds.

11 o'clock came, and I was taking my fifteen minute break. I looked up and Dennis was coming in the door, his shift was from 11am to 8pm.

"Hey, Day," said Dennis, while smiling at me. "You look good in your new uniform."

"Thank you," I said, smiling back at him.

"Day, you're very beautiful, and I would like to take you out to lunch or dinner one day."

I smiled and said, "Dennis I would like that."

Just as we were talking, James came over, "Dennis, you need to clock in for your shift."

Dennis didn't know that James and I were living in the same house. He didn't know that the man was a coward who beats me like I'm a man in the streets. No one in here knew that James was beating me because I hid every scare with blush so no one could not tell. And on the days that I had a black eye, I would call off work.

Break was over and I was told by Bruce to take orders in the drive-thru which was right next to Dennis, who was the drive-thru window cashier. James looked sick, but, while he was watching me, Sheila was watching him. I was laughing on the inside as James couldn't do his work, being too busy watching me, and Sheila couldn't do hers as she was too busy watching James. I didn't say anything to Dennis even though he was trying to talk to me. I knew once we got into the car, he was going to hit me, but I didn't care because I felt good about myself today.

It was now 1:30pm and it was time for lunch. I sat at the table by the window, where I always sit. James came up to me and started asking me questions about Dennis. I tried to tell him that I hadn't talked to Dennis this whole time, but James started to raise his voice at me. Bruce, the general manager, walked over and asked if everything was alright. He knew we were dating and also knew that James was super controlling, but he didn't know he beat me. We told Bruce everything was fine, and he told us to be calm around the customers.

Eventually, our shift finished. Before we left, Bruce called me in the office and asked me about James. He had seen how James would grab me outside when he thought nobody was watching. Bruce asked me if I needed any help. He told me to be careful, but I knew I was stuck with James, at least until I was 18.

I walked out of the office and saw James standing there, looking at me with bloodshot eyes, so I knew that there would be a fight, either when we got home, or while we were in the car. I grabbed my things and went to the car. Behind me, James asked, "what were you talking about, Day?"

I lied and said that he was going over some paperwork with me on how to make the money drop offs. I already knew how to do it, but James didn't know that. We got in the car, and he said, "Day, you better not be lying to me and you better not tell nobody what is going on in my house. It's not anyone's business what is going on behind closed doors."

"James, I didn't say anything to Bruce about what was going on, I promise you I didn't." To my surprise, he believed me.

When I got to the daycare, Lance Jr's teacher sang my baby's praises. He never cried, only when he was hungry or needed a diaper change. Most people loved little Lance Jr, at least, everyone but my mother and James. It was funny, because my mother loved children, but she had changed ever since she got addicted to drugs. When I got back to the car with Lance Jr in hand, I saw James on his phone laughing. As I got close to the car, I heard him say, "I love you, I'll talk to you later."

Now I'm assuming that he was talking to Sheila. I knew James hated it when I asked him about his life, but I couldn't help myself. I asked him who he was talking to. He told me it was his mother, which was strange as I never met nor heard of his mother.

As we pulled up to the house, I noticed that he wasn't getting out of the car. I took the baby out and walked up to the door and all I heard were the tires speeding off. I ran in the house, got myself together, and made some calls to the GED teacher as he had called and left a message on my phone, telling me there was a spot open for me. I had it all figured out. When I went to the school for the 1st time to sign up for the classes, I explained my situation. I told them I was in an abusive relationship and didn't want James to know that I was taking the classes.

"Good afternoon, Daytona. This is Mr. Thomas from the GED program. I've emailed you material for you to study and I'll give you two weeks to study. Then, we can sign you up to take the test."

"Perfect," I said and hung up. Me and the baby went down to the library so I could get the pages printed off my phone. I knew that James wasn't coming back in no time as soon as he was out with Sheila or, his mother, I thought, laughing to myself. After I got that done, I called Child Services and got signed up for programs that would help me get housing and my brothers away from my mother.

On my way home I stopped to get something to eat as I was not allowed to cook anything in James' house. If he's not there, I have to wait for him to come and make food for us. Since I wasn't sure when he was coming home, I grabbed something to eat. When I got home, I gave Lance Jr a bath, took a shower myself and started watching television. I looked at the time, and it was 12 AM. We got off work at 4 PM, and it is now 12 AM and James still wasn't home. As I was about to go upstairs, I heard the door open and then close. It was James, and he was talking on the phone. I heard him talk about having a good time and how he should do this again. He hung up, and when he saw me standing there, looking at him, he asked why I was still up. I told him I wasn't tired yet, only for him to pass me going up the steps. He pushed me out of the way, telling me to sleep in the other room. He didn't want me in the same bed with him. I said, "alright, James. I will sleep in the room with my son."

Next thing I knew, he was grabbing me by my hair and pulling me up the steps, down the hall, and into the bedroom. He repeatedly kicked me in my head and in my side while I screamed for him to stop. He dragged me on the bed and said, "this is where you want to sleep."

He slammed me on the bed and told me I better not get out of bed until the next morning. I laid there crying holding my stomach as he yelled at me to shut up.

I was in the worst place I've ever been in, I wanted my mother so badly, I wanted to call her and tell her that this was all her fault. I was in this relationship because of her. I knew it wasn't really her fault, but it was because she put me out at an early age, and now my son and I are living with a man that doesn't love me or my son. I wanted my girls or someone to come and get me out of this relationship as I was too scared to walk away from this man myself.

Chapter Seven

So, two weeks passed, and I was ready to take my GED test. James was off with Sheila somewhere, so that gave me the perfect opportunity to go to the GED program and take my test. I managed to pass with flying colors; I was so happy that tears came down my eyes, I was getting closer to my goal. I was turning eighteen in ten months, so I was excited. I would soon be reunited with my brothers.

On my way home, I got a call from Brianna, telling me they have my two little brothers at her house as my mother was in the hospital. She told me I needed to come over to her house. I called James but there was no answer, I called again and was sent to voicemail. I left him a message, telling him that I had to go over to the hospital so I could see my mother and get my little brothers and bring them back to the house until my mother got out of the hospital.

The baby and I got over to Brianna's house within an hour. As I was getting off the bus, James called me, asking where I was and what I had sent him on voice mail. I told him about my mother being sick, and that I had gone to take care of her at the hospital. I went on to ask if my brothers could stay at James' house with us, and he got really quiet. In the end, he told me he was willing to let them stay with us, and I thanked him before hanging up.

"Brianna, what happened?" I asked.

"Day I don't know; Dakota ran over here screaming for help. We called the police and they told us that your mother had had a heart attack and needed immediate resuscitation."

I started crying, telling Brianna that my mother and I weren't very close ever since I got pregnant. My girls went with me and my brothers to the hospital and when we got there, I saw my mother hooked up to all kinds of machines. I asked Julie if she could take my little brothers to get something to eat while I talked with the doctors.

After speaking with the doctors, I called my aunt and my grandmother to tell them what was going on with my mother. My grandmother and my mother didn't get along because she had had me at a young age, although they would call each other every now and then to make sure that we were okay. After Julie came back from getting the boys something to eat, I sat my brothers down and explained to them what was going on with our mother. I explained that her condition can change at any time, but right now, she is in critical condition. I took them in the room to see her one by one, Dakota took it the hardest, he started crying, asking if she was going to die. I really didn't know what to say because I didn't know myself. I hugged my brothers and we cried together, I looked up and I saw my aunt and grandmother walking in the ER, so I called them over.

"Day, what happened? Was it the drugs she had been taking?" asked my grandmother.

"I don't know what happened, I wasn't there, my mother put me out last year when I got pregnant with my son."

My grandmother didn't know that I had a baby because she never came around or called either of us to see how we were doing. Even if she did, I'm sure my mother never told her what was going on. That was the rule in my mother's house: never tell what goes on in her house.

Grandma asked for my son, and Brianna brought him over. To my surprise, my grandmother took him in her arms and held him tight. As everyone was in the waiting room, the doctor came out to talk to us.

The doctor told my family and myself that my mother had pneumonia and a few other problems, and they are going to keep her in the hospital until they can get the fluids out of her lungs. James kept calling me and leaving threatening messages on my answer machine. I didn't want to hear him right now and I didn't want to argue right now so I didn't respond to his calls or messages. I knew we would fight when

I got home, but I didn't care at this point. My mother is sick in a hospital bed with tubes in her mouth and arms.

My grandma asked where I lived, and I told her a bit about James.

"Well, are your brothers allowed to come there? Because if not, I can keep them at my house until your mother gets better."

I decided to refuse my grandmother's offer as I did not want her to end up calling Child Protective Services on my mother who came home from the hospital a week later. I kept my brothers for another week just to let her get some rest. It was very hard having my brothers there with James beating me. He didn't do it in front of them, only while they were in school or asleep at night. I didn't know how much longer I could take this man beating me. My ribs were hurting for a couple of days and I didn't know if they were broken from him kicking me there the other night. I had a black and blue mark across my back and my ribs. I was scared to go get checked up at the hospital because I was afraid of the hospital calling the police and locking James up. I suffered bloody noses, blows to my head, my ribs and back, but I still didn't want to leave. James would come to me and tell me he's sorry and that he will never do it again, but he did it repeatedly. I wanted to tell my girls, my mother, I even wanted to tell my grandmother, but I couldn't. I was afraid of them judging me. I knew what James was doing to me was wrong, but he gave me his home for free, so I couldn't leave yet.

I called my mother to see how she was doing, and if it was okay to take the boys home, I really didn't want them to stay here much longer.

James may have not said anything because he was barely here but I knew he had a problem with them staying here. One day he asked when my mother was coming home from the hospital, and that he was tired of my brothers being here. So, I knew it was time for me to take them home.

James had been staying out lately. I knew he and Sheila had to be seeing each other as every time I came to work, she would give me these dirty looks and laugh with her friends. Now she is older than me, but if needed to, I will hurt that lady and think nothing about it. But I am just not into confrontation, especially not over a man.

The day was over, and it was time for us to get off work. I was surprised that James was coming home today. Him and Sheila must have got into a fight. As we pulled up to the door, James asked if Dennis and I were seeing each other. He would always find a way where he will start with me, just so he can put his hands on me. Mind you, Dennis works from 11am to 8pm and he works back where they make the food. But I wasn't going to stop talking to Dennis just because James wanted me to.

"James, why do you ask that?" I asked him. He didn't say anything, just got out of the car and walked into the house. I had another 2 hours before it was time for me to pick the baby up so James pulled me in the house, threw me to the floor, and started choking me, asking me to tell him the truth. I stopped breathing for a second and he let me go and walked upstairs. I laid there, trying to get my breath back. I heard myself crying for my mother, I really needed her right now. James came running back down the steps yelling.

"Why are you calling out for your mom?! She can't help you; she doesn't even want you, she never wanted you, that's why she threw you out of the house." He called me all kinds of names and told me I wasn't a good mother to my son, that I would be nothing without him. I have always been a good person to everyone, including James.

I got up to get myself together to go and get my son, but James pushed me back on the floor and once again he raped me, he bit me all on my back to the point that he broke my skin. I knew I needed to go to the hospital to get a tetanus shot. "James, please stop," I cried out, this man was a totally different person, he didn't hear anything I was saying to him, he just kept on abusing me, I just lay there crying until he was done. Once he got up, he spit in my face and told me to clean myself up so we can go and pick up my son. I couldn't move as my back was throbbing from the pain.

I finally got up after laying there for ten minutes, I looked at myself in the mirror, crying. After I took my shower, I put some ointment on my back, at least, the places that I could reach. It burned so bad that I wanted to scream. Getting dressed was even worse as my shirt rubbed up on my back, which made it hurt more.

When we got to the daycare center, I pulled on the door to go get my son, but James grabbed my arm and said that he will go in and get him. He didn't want me telling them what he did to me.

"Day you want me to go to jail?" he asked, while squeezing my arm real tight.

"No," I said, and he got out of the car. I wanted so badly to call my mother and tell her what was going on. But on the other hand, I loved this man no matter what he was doing to me. This man gave me and my son a place to stay, rent free. He got me a job, how could I leave this man. I was blind to all the things that he was doing to me and only focused on what he did for me, which I knew was wrong. I had seen all the things my mother went through with my father, the beatings that he gave her, and in my eyes, I thought this was okay, because my mother never left my father. He just went to jail, and when he came home, he was right back in the house with us, making another baby. My phone was ringing, and it was Brianna but I didn't answer because I didn't want James to see me on the phone and start asking more questions.

Chapter Eight

Summer was approaching real soon, and I was happy because at the end of the year I will be turning eighteen. I had saved over twenty thousand dollars so I can get an apartment for my brothers, my son and me. Plus, I had passed my GED test, I'm a manager at my job and had gotten a raise for two dollars around two weeks ago. Obviously, I didn't tell James that I got the raise. Bruce figured out what was going on and told me that, although it was none of his business, he could give me some phone numbers to call for abused women. I took the numbers, but I never called them. As the months went on, James abused me over and over, I called out of work for a week as I had a black eye. My son was now a year old and he asked so many questions about my eye.

James barely came home at night, and when he did it, there was nothing but arguments and fights. I would ask him about being with Sheila every night, and he would tell me it's none of my business where he had been. He would call me ugly and say things about my son's father, but that didn't bother me. What bothered me was that I was in a relationship with a man that physically, mentally, emotionally, and sexually abused me and that I was too scared to walk away from it.

On April 27th, I had an appointment with the social worker that was handling my case for custody of my brothers. I was so excited that the social worker told me that, since I was turning eighteen at the end of the year and had done everything that was asked of me, I can start looking for a place to move. I called my girls and told them the good news, Brianna hit me with some bad news in return, my mother wasn't doing too well. I knew the condition of my mother, she had full blown AIDS, heart problems and the doctors wanted her to stop doing drugs. But it was none of my girls' business what was going on with my mother. I was sure Brianna's mother already told her the news and Brianna told Julie. But that was the least of my worries right now, I had to go and help my mother take care of my brothers.

When I got home, I called James and told him about my mom and how I would have to go take care of her and my brothers. Well the conversation didn't go the way I wanted it to go and James accused me of cheating. He said I was going to town to see my baby's father. He called me all kinds of names, told me I was stupid and that I will amount to nothing. I just listened to him belittle me over and over, with tears in my eyes.

I didn't care about what would happen to me. I had to go see my mother, I needed to make sure that she was alright. When I got there, she was lying on the couch sleeping, Dallas was lying beside her, just watching her. I couldn't see my mother like this, but I had to be strong for my brothers, so I held back my tears.

I took the boys in their room and told them to watch little Lance while I gave my mother a bath, fed her, and did her hair for her. I gave her medicine and helped her lay back down so she can get some rest. I stayed with them until the boys went to sleep. I asked Brianna if she could keep an eye on the house and the boys.

As I was walking to the bus stop a car pulled up on me. It was James, telling me to get in the car. At first, I just looked at him, all I could see was blood in his eyes. I knew I couldn't deny him. After I put my son in the car seat, trying not to wake him up, James jumped out of the car, ran over to me, and started punching me. I covered my face, so he punched me in my stomach. I fell to the ground and once again, he kicked me in my back and side. He started choking me, yelling, "where is he, Day, where is your baby's father at?"

He picked me up and threw me in the car, and as he did that, I hit my head on the door. Once he got in the car, he started asking me questions about where I had been and who I was with. I kept telling him how my mother was really sick and that I was there with her and my brothers, but he didn't believe anything I was saying.

When we got home, James beat me so badly that he put me in the hospital. I had two broken ribs, a broken nose, broken arm, and both of my eyes were black. When I finally woke up, Brianna, my grandmother and my aunt were sitting in the room crying. I was in a coma for two weeks because of James kicking me in my head. I really couldn't talk that well because my jaw was wired as well, but I managed to ask for my son and my mother. I was told that while my son was fine, my mother had died a week ago.

I laid there, with tears in my eyes, thinking how I never told my mother that I loved her. My aunt also told me that James was in jail and that what he did to me was the same thing he did to his wife, who ended up dying from him punching her in the head. My aunt told me that they gave him 20 years with no parole, I was glad that all the beatings were over. But I wasn't glad that I lost my mother while I was laid up in the hospital in a coma, all because of James.

A week later, I got out of the hospital. I had to go and stay with my grandmother until my house was ready. The state gave me a ten thousand dollar grant for the down payment on my house. I was moving into a nice house, and I ended up letting my girls move in with me. My grandmother lived 20 minutes away and my aunt lived half an hour away from where I moved to.

Needless to say, I got my GED, my own house, and am legally my brothers' guardian. I bought myself a car, and am the General Manager at my new job. Dennis and I are seeing each other as a couple now. I survived all that I've been through, and I wouldn't wish this on anyone.

The End

My name is Victoria Hall. At the age of 53, I accomplished one of my dreams, and that was to write books. When I was 16 years old, I wanted to write novels, but the streets, drugs, and boyfriends had me. So I put my dreams to the side. I always told my children that one day I was going to write a book.

www.ingramcontent.com/pod-product-compliance
Lightning Source LLC
Chambersburg PA
CBHW071358200726
48294CB00004B/1213